Pinkie's Pies

Based on the
My Little Pony TV series

Picture words

Pinkie Pie Rainbow Dash

Caretaker Pony

the Wonderbolts

Ladybird  Readers

Pinkie's Pies

'e

Series Editor: Sorrel Pitts
Text adapted by Sorrel Pitts
Activities written by Naomi Rainbow
Song lyrics by Wardour Studios

LADYBIRD BOOKS

UK | USA | Canada | Ireland | Australia
India | New Zealand | South Africa

Ladybird Books is part of the Penguin Random House group of companies
whose addresses can be found at global.penguinrandomhouse.com.
www.penguin.co.uk   www.puffin.co.uk   www.ladybird.co.uk

First published 2021
001

Licensed by:

Printed in China

A CIP catalogue record for this book is available from the British Library

ISBN: 978-0-241-47545-4

All correspondence to:
Ladybird Books
Penguin Random House Children's
One Embassy Gardens, 8 Viaduct Gardens, London SW11 7BW

MIX
Paper from
responsible sources
FSC® C018179

Applejack

pie

point

trash can

sneeze

Pinkie Pie made a fruit pie for Rainbow Dash.

'Oh . . . thank you!"
Rainbow Dash said.

"I LOVE your pies."

Then, Rainbow Dash
pointed.

"Look behind you!" she said.

"What is it?" asked
Pinkie Pie.

"Don't worry!" said Rainbow Dash. "This pie is GREAT!"

"Take it home," said Pinkie Pie.

Then, Pinkie Pie saw
the Caretaker Pony with
a trash can.

"That's my pie!" she thought.

"Does Rainbow Dash eat my pies . . . or not?" she thought.

"First, I made a pie for her birthday . . ."

*"Thank you! I love your pies,"
said Rainbow Dash.*

"Look behind you!"

"That pie was GREAT!"

"Then, I made her some ice-cream pies . . ."

"I love your ice-cream pies," said Rainbow Dash.

"Look behind you!"

"Those pies were GREAT!"

"I need answers," said
Pinkie Pie.

"Does Rainbow Dash eat my pies?" she asked the Wonderbolts.

"We don't know," they said.

"Does Rainbow Dash eat my pies?" Pinkie Pie asked Applejack.

"I don't know," said Applejack.

Pinkie Pie was very
angry now.

"Give me those apples!"
she said.

Then, she made an apple pie for Rainbow Dash.

"I LOVE your apple pies,"
said Rainbow Dash.

Rainbow Dash
gave Pinkie
Pie some
flowers.

Pinkie Pie
closed her
eyes . . .

and sneezed!

"The pie was GREAT!"
said Rainbow Dash.

"Here are lots of pies," said
Pinkie Pie. "Now, eat them!"

"Look, pies!" said Rainbow
Dash to the ponies.

"Those pies were GREAT!"
she said.

"You DON'T eat my pies!" said Pinkie Pie.

"I'm sorry. I don't like pies," said Rainbow Dash.

"You are not my friend!" said Pinkie Pie. She went home.

Rainbow Dash was sad.

She went to Pinkie Pie's house.

"Look, I made this horrible pie," she told Pinkie Pie.

"I'm eating it because I'm sorry."

"Don't eat it!" said Pinkie Pie. "You don't like pies, but you wanted me to be happy. I understand."

"Let's be friends again!"
said Rainbow Dash.

Activities

The key below describes the skills practiced in each activity.

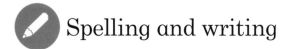 Spelling and writing

Reading

Speaking

Listening*

Critical thinking

Singing*

Preparation for the Cambridge Young Learners exams

*To complete these activities, listen to the audio downloads available at **www.ladybirdeducation.co.uk**

1 **Match the words to the pictures.**

1 Pinkie Pie   (a)

2 Rainbow Dash   (b)

3 Applejack   (c)

4 Caretaker Pony   (d)

2 **Ask and answer the questions with a friend.** ⬤ ⬤

1 *What is in the pie?*

The pie has fruit in it.

2 Do you like pies? Why? / Why not?

3 What foods do you like?

4 What foods do you not like?

3 Write the correct verbs.

1 Pinkie Pie **(make)** ...._made_.......... a pie.

2 Pinkie Pie **(give)** .... the pie to Rainbow Dash.

3 "Thank you!" **(say)** .... Rainbow Dash.

4 Then, Rainbow Dash **(point)** .... behind Pinkie Pie.

5 Pinkie Pie **(look)** .... behind her.

4 Circle the correct sentences.

1

   a Pinkie Pie made a fruit pie.

   b Pinkie Pie made a cake.

2

   a Then, Rainbow Dash danced.

   b Then, Rainbow Dash pointed.

3

   a Caretaker Pony did not have the pie.

   b Caretaker Pony had the pie.

4

   a "That's my pie!" she thought.

   b "That's my pie!" she said.

Write the missing letters.

ie   ow   sh   in   rt

1    p i e

2    t r a _____

3    b i _____ h d a y

4    t h _____ k

5    f l _____ e r s

6 **Listen, and** ✓ **the boxes.**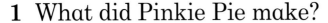

1 What did Pinkie Pie make?

a    b 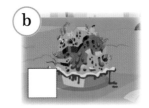   c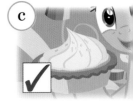

2 What did Pinkie Pie have?

a    b    c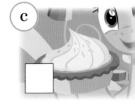

3 Who did Pinkie Pie ask?

a    b    c

4 Who did Pinkie Pie see?

a    b 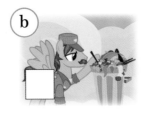   c

7 Who said this?

| the Wonderbolts | Applejack | Pinkie Pie | Rainbow Dash |

1 "We don't know,"

said ....the Wonderbolts.....

2 "I don't know,"

said ....

3 "Give me those apples!"

said ....

4 "The pie was GREAT!"

said ....

5 "Here are lots of pies,"

said ....

8 Write *on, in, behind,* or *in front of.*

1 The picture is _____on_____ the wall.

2 The pie is _____ the wall.

3 Rainbow Dash is _____ the window.

4 The flowers are _____ Rainbow Dash.

9 Find the words.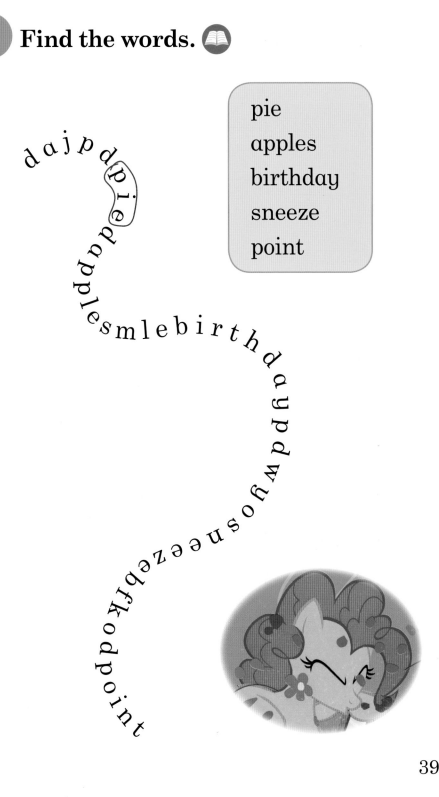

pie
apples
birthday
sneeze
point

dajpdpie
dappplesmlebirthdaypdwyosneezebfkodpoint

Circle the correct pictures.

1 You can eat this.

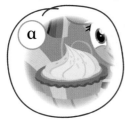 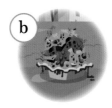 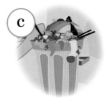

2 The fruit pie was in this.

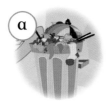  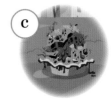

3 These are fruit.

 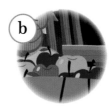 

4 You put this on your wall.

  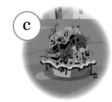

11 Circle the correct answers.

1 Did Applejack know if Rainbow Dash was eating the pies?
  a No, Applejack did not know.
  b Yes, Applejack knew.

2 Was Pinkie Pie very happy then?
  a No, Pinkie Pie was very tired then.
  b No, Pinkie Pie was very angry then.

3 Why did Pinkie Pie want apples?
  a To make apple juice.
  b To make an apple pie.

12 **Look at the picture and read the questions. Write the answers.**

1 What colour is Rainbow Dash?

She is .... blue ....

2 What is Rainbow Dash holding?

She is holding lots of ....

3 Who is Rainbow Dash talking to?

She is talking to ....

3 **Read the text and circle the correct answers.**

1 Rainbow Dash went to Pinkie Pie's
   a kitchen.
   b house.

2 "Look, I made this . . . pie,"
   Rainbow Dash told Pinkie Pie.
   a horrible
   b nice

3 Pinkie Pie said, "You don't like pies,
   but you wanted me to be . . .
   a sad."
   b happy."

4 "Let's be . . . again!" said
   Rainbow Dash.
   a friends
   b angry

14 Read the questions.
Write the answers.

1 Does Rainbow Dash like pies?

No, Rainbow Dash does not like pies.

2 Does Rainbow Dash eat the horrible pie?

3 Does Pinkie Pie understand?

4 Is Pinkie Pie angry?

5 Talk about the two pictures with a friend. How are they different? Use the words in the box.

Pinkie Pie   pie   Rainbow Dash
lots   happy   sad   angry

In picture a, Pinkie Pie has a pie. In picture b, Rainbow Dash has lots of pies.

16 Look at the pictures.
Tell the story to your friend.

1  2

3  4

Pinkie Pie makes a pie . . .

Sing the song.

"Look behind you!" Rainbow Dash said.
"Thank you! Thank you, Pinkie Pie!
Look behind you! This pie is great!
I love your ice-cream pies!"

"I need answers," said Pinkie Pie.
"Does she eat my pies?"
Pinkie was very angry now.
She said, "You DON'T eat my pies!"

"Sorry, I don't like pies!"
Rainbow Dash was sad.
She made a really horrible pie
to eat because she was sorry.

"Don't!" said Pinkie. "You don't like pies.
I understand. You wanted me to be happy."
"Let's be friends!" said Rainbow Dash.
"Let's be friends! Let's be friends again!"

Visit www.ladybirdeducation.co.uk
for more FREE Ladybird Readers resources

✓ Digital edition of every title

✓ Audio tracks (US/UK)

✓ Answer keys

✓ Lesson plans

✓ Role-plays

✓ Classroom display material

✓ Flashcards

✓ User guides

Register and sign up to the newsletter to receive your FREE classroom resource pack!

To access the audio and digital versions of this book:

1 Go to www.ladybirdeducation.co.uk
2 Click "Unlock book"
3 Enter the code below

KCVsAaNS5w